SUSAN LEHR

A Michael Neugebauer Book.
Copyright © 1991 Neugebauer Press, Salzburg, Austria.
Original title: Abiel et la Santé Nuit.
Published and distributed in USA by Picture Book Studio, Saxonville, MA.
Printed in Hong Kong.
10 9 8 7 6 5 4 3 2 1

Library of Congress Cataloging-in-Publication Data
Tharlet, Eve
[Abiel et la santé nuit. English]
Simon and the holy night / by Eve Tharlet; illustrated by Eve Tharlet;
translated by Andrew Clements.
p. cm.
Translation of: Abiel et la santé nuit.
Summary: Relates how a little shepherd boy comes to witness the events surrounding the birth of Jesus Christ.
ISBN 0-88708-185-1 : $14.95
[1. Shepherds–Fiction. 2. Jesus Christ–Nativity–Fiction.] I. Title.
PZ7.T326Si   1991
[E]–dc20   91–15636

Ask your bookseller for these other *Picture Book Studio* books illustrated by Eve Tharlet:
Dizzy From Fools by M.L.Miller
The Princess and the Pea by H.C.Andersen
The Wishing Table by The Brothers Grimm
The Brave Little Tailor by the Brothers Grimm
And these books written and illustrated by Eve Tharlet:
Little Pig, Big Trouble
Christmas Won't Wait

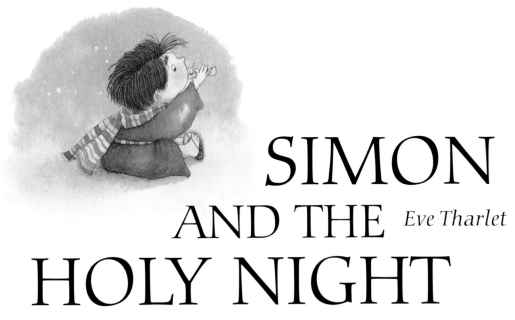

SIMON
AND THE *Eve Tharlet*
HOLY NIGHT

translated by Andrew Clements

Picture Book Studio

Simon sat there on the cold ground.
It was late, and it was time to lead the sheep home.
But one of the lambs had wandered off, and it was still missing.

"My father's going to be angry with me," he thought.

As he sat there, a man came along the road.
He was leading a donkey, and his wife sat on its back.
The man stopped and asked why Simon looked so sad.

"I've lost a lamb," said Simon, "and it's going to be a cold night."
The stranger smiled. He reached into the folds of his robe
and pulled out the little lamb, nice and warm.

"I found him shivering by the footpath…"
And he put the lamb into the little shepherd's arms.

Simon thanked the man and his wife again and again,
and then walked along the road with them.
The man's name was Joseph and he explained that they
were going to stay in the town for several days.

"We need to find a place to stay. You see, Mary is going to have a baby."

"And I think it will be soon," she said softly.

"But there are so many people in Bethlehem right now," said Simon.
"If you can't find a room, there's a stable over in that direction,
and hardly anyone ever goes there."

Then Simon said good-bye, and left them at the edge of town.

Joseph and Mary went to the inn,
and then from house to house.
But no one had a place for them to stay.
It was getting late,
and Mary was tired from the journey.

"Let's stop looking for a room, Joseph.
We'll find nothing here.
Take me to the little shepherd's stable."

So Joseph led the donkey away.

Later that night, Simon couldn't get to sleep.
He lay in his bed, and he kept thinking and thinking
about Joseph and Mary. He wondered if they'd found a place to stay.

The night was clear and bright, and he looked out his window.
In the distance he could see the stable. A little light was shining.

"I bet that's where they are!" he thought.

Simon got out of bed, quietly slipped out of his house,
and ran to the stable. He didn't know why,
but he felt like he just had to go and see his friends again, right now.
When he came near, he heard a child crying.
"The baby was born," he whispered.

He tapped at the stable door, and Joseph invited him inside.

Mary held the baby close to her.
The mother and child were surrounded by a beautiful warm light,
and Simon couldn't see where it came from.

Simon was amazed.
He stood very still because he felt like something important
was happening here.

"Go over closer," Joseph told him. "This is Jesus."

Simon looked at the baby. Then he took off
the woolen shepherd's scarf he always wore,
and handed it to Mary. "This is to wrap Jesus in."

Then he pulled his wooden flute from his pocket
and gave it to Joseph. "This is to help put him to sleep at night."

As Mary tucked the scarf around the baby,
little Jesus opened his eyes and smiled at Simon.

But suddenly a dog barked outside, and there were voices
and singing, and the sound of sheep coming toward them.

Simon and Joseph stepped outside, and they were astonished to see men and women, shepherds and farmers, and even some children—all coming to the stable from every direction. It was the middle of the night, but it felt like a celebration. Some of the people carried flowers or fruit, others brought cheese and milk.

One of the shepherds spoke up and said, "An angel came to us from heaven, and lighted up the sky. He told us that the savior of the world was born this night in a stable, and that he was sleeping in a manger. We had to come and see, and here we are!"

Joseph let them come into the stable.
They all knelt down quietly in front of Jesus,
and one of the women sang a little lullaby.

Simon slipped away quietly and went back to his house.
He was very happy.

Later that week, three wise men arrived from the East.
They had seen a new star in the sky,
a sign that a king was going to be born.

They brought rich gifts, and said:
"We have come to worship the newborn king.
We followed his star, and it led us here."

In the days and weeks that followed, Simon thought a lot about all that had happened that night at the stable.

He thought about Mary and Joseph and the little Jesus, and he knew that he would never, ever forget them.